LIONS
IN A FLAP

A book about feeling worried

Written by Sue Graves

Illustrated by Trevor Dunton

W
FRANKLIN WATTS
LONDON·SYDNEY

Lion was always worrying. He worried about **everything!** He worried if he was late for school.

He worried if he was early, too.

Lion even worried about getting all his sums right… and he was really good at sums. Lion always got in a flap when he worried. He felt hot and dizzy. His tummy quivered and his knees knocked. It was a **horrid** feeling.

On Friday, Miss Bird had some exciting news. She said it was the **Big Day Out** in two weeks' time. She said this year they were all going to Jungle Land and Mr Croc was going to take them in the school minibus. Everyone clapped and cheered. Jungle Land was the best theme park in the jungle. **Everyone was excited**. Everyone, that is, except Lion – and he began to worry.

All through football, Lion worried about the Big Day Out. He worried about getting to Jungle Land. What if the minibus **broke down**? What if they couldn't get to Jungle Land at all? That would be **dreadful**! Lion got in such a flap that he let in lots of goals.

On Monday, Lion worried that it might **rain** on the Big Day Out. That would be no fun at all. And what if it rained so hard that Jungle Land flooded and had to close? That would be **terrible**! Lion got in such a flap that he knocked paint all over Hippo's picture.

Monkey and Hippo were worried about Lion.
They asked him if he was all right. But Lion did
not tell them he was worried about the Big Day
Out. He was afraid they would laugh at him.

The next day, Lion worried about **the rides** at Jungle Land. What if he was too small to go on them… or too big? That would be **awful!** Lion got in such a flap that he knocked all the pencils and books on to the floor.

"Lion's in a flap!" everyone said.

Miss Bird took Lion outside to **calm down**.

Miss Bird asked Lion what was wrong. He told her all his worries about the Big Day Out. Miss Bird listened carefully. She told him that when she felt worried she always took a **deep breath**. Lion took a deep breath. He felt a **little better**.

14

Then Miss Bird told him to think about all the **good things** that might happen on the Big Day Out, instead of all the bad things. Lion had a good think.

He thought about the minibus. Mr Croc looked after it very well. He always checked the tyres. He always checked the oil. The minibus might not break down at all. Lion felt **much better**.

Then he thought about the weather. There were no clouds in the sky and it hadn't rained for weeks and weeks. It might not rain at all on the Big Day Out. Jungle Land might not flood and then it would stay open **all day**! Lion felt a **lot better**.

Then Miss Bird told Lion that everyone gets worried sometimes. She said Lion could always talk about his worries with his friends. Lion said that Monkey and Hippo were his **best** friends. Miss Bird said they would be very good friends to talk to if he felt worried again. Lion felt **much, much better**.

On Friday, it was the Big Day Out.
The minibus did not break down at all.

And it only rained in the afternoon when everyone was on the Water Ride, so it **didn't matter** anyway.

Lion was a bit too big to go on the Runaway Train, but he **didn't mind** at all. He went on the Roaring Rocket instead and that was **even more fun**!

Then Miss Bird looked at her watch. She said there was just enough time for everyone to go on **the Big Drop**. The Big Drop was the highest, fastest and scariest ride in Jungle Land.

Everyone was very excited. But Lion began to worry. What if the ride was too high and too fast? What if it was **too scary**? Worse still, what if he could not sit next to his friends? That would be **really horrid**!

Then Lion remembered what Miss Bird had told him. He took a **deep breath**. He felt a bit better. He told Monkey and Hippo his worries. Monkey said the ride could not be too high, too fast or too scary because everyone was having **lots** of fun on it. Then Hippo said that they would all sit together so that Lion felt nice and safe. Lion felt **much better**.

The Big Drop was very high and very fast… and it was **very scary**! Lion felt hot and dizzy. His tummy quivered and his knees knocked. But Lion wasn't worried. He wasn't worried at all. He was having a **brilliant** time!

A note about sharing this book

The *Behaviour Matters* series has been developed to provide a starting point for further discussion on children's behaviour both in relation to themselves and others. The series is set in the jungle with animal characters reflecting typical behaviour traits often seen in young children.

Lion's in a Flap

This story explores some of the typical worries experienced by children. The book aims to encourage children to develop strategies for dealing with anxiety. It also looks at ways in which others might help someone to overcome their concerns.

How to use the book

The book is designed for adults to share with either an individual child, or a group of children, and as a starting point for discussion.

The book also provides visual support and repeated words and phrases to build reading confidence.

Before reading the story

Choose a time to read when you and the children are relaxed and have time to share the story.

Spend time looking at the illustrations and talk about what the book might be about before reading it together.

Encourage children to employ a phonics first approach to tackling new words by sounding the words out.

After reading, talk about the book with the children:

- Talk about the story with the children. Encourage them to retell the events in chronological order.

- Talk about Lion's worries. Ask the children if they worry about similar things. Invite them to share their worries with the others. Take the opportunity to point out that many people worry about the same things.

- Ask the children to explain how they feel when they get worried. Do they get butterflies in their tummies when faced with something new or different? Do they feel shaky and uncertain? Ask them how they handle these feelings. Have any developed their own strategies for dealing with these physical features of anxiety?

- As a group, ask the children to take a deep breath and exhale slowly. Ask them how this makes them feel. Do they feel calmer? Point out that this is a good strategy for dealing with anxiety.

- Extend this by talking about other ways of calming themselves or others who feel anxious. Who would the children confide in? Would they prefer to share their worries with friends or with parents or carers? Why?

- Place the children into groups of three or four. Ask them to find one particular worry that they all share, e.g. worrying about school work, worrying about friendships etc. Ask each group to discuss how they could overcome their concerns.

- Invite the groups to return and ask a spokesperson from each group to talk about their findings. Encourage the others to comment on the concerns raised and the resolutions suggested.

Franklin Watts
First published in Great Britain in 2016 by The Watts Publishing Group

Series Editor: Jackie Hamley
Series Designer: Cathryn Gilbert

A CIP catalogue record for this book is available
from the British Library.

ISBN 978 1 4451 4248 7 (pbk)
ISBN 978 1 4451 4226 5 (library ebook)

Printed in China

Franklin Watts
An imprint of
Hachette Children's Group
Part of The Watts Publishing Group
Carmelite House
50 Victoria Embankment
London EC4Y 0DZ

An Hachette UK Company
www.hachette.co.uk

www.franklinwatts.co.uk

FSC
www.fsc.org
MIX
Paper from
responsible sources
FSC® C104740